THE SHU-TORUN WAR: VOLUME 5

It is a time of unrest. Following the destruction of the Death Star, Darth Vader has shown zero mercy to any rebel sympathizers.

The newly appointed Queen Trios has found herself in the middle of a war on her home planet of Shu-Torun. While she tries to comply with Vader's orders, her people resist. Angered by the Empire's continued mistreatment, they have fought back, recruiting the aid of Cylo to bring an end to Vader's brutality. Alas, no secret is kept from Vader for long, who has suspected betrayal and prepared accordingly.

Meanwhile, Vader's secret ally, Dr. Aphra, remains in rebel hands. He has issued a bounty for her recovery, dead or alive, and will stop at nothing to regain control....

KIERON GILLEN
Writer

SALVADOR LARROCA
Artist

EDGAR DELGADO
Colorist

VC's JOE CARAMAGNA
Letterer

MARK BROOKS
Cover Artist

HEATHER ANTOS
Assistant Editor

JORDAN D. WHITE
Editor

C.B. CEBULSKI
Executive Editor

AXEL ALONSO
Editor In Chief

JOE QUESADA
Chief Creative Officer

DAN BUCKLEY
Publisher

For Lucasfilm:
Senior Editor **FRANK PARISI**
Creative Director **MICHAEL SIGLAIN**
Lucasfilm Story Group **RAYNE ROBERTS, PABLO HIDALGO, LELAND CHEE, MATT MARTIN**

Spotlight

ABDOPUBLISHING.COM

Reinforced library bound edition published in 2019 by Spotlight,
a division of ABDO, PO Box 398166, Minneapolis, Minnesota 55439.
Spotlight produces high-quality reinforced library bound editions for
schools and libraries. Published by agreement with Marvel Characters, Inc.

Printed in the United States of America, North Mankato, Minnesota.
042018
092018

THIS BOOK CONTAINS
RECYCLED MATERIALS

STAR WARS © & TM 2018 LUCASFILM LTD.

PUBLISHER'S CATALOGING-IN-PUBLICATION DATA

Names: Gillen, Kieron, author. | Yu, Leinil Francis; Alanguilan, Gerry; Keith, Jason;
   Larroca, Salvador; Delgado, Edgar, illustrators.
Title: The Shu-Torun War / writer: Kieron Gillen; art: Leinil Francis Yu, Gerry
   Alanguilan, Jason Keith, Salvador Larroca and Edgar Delgado.
Description: Reinforced library bound edition. | Minneapolis, MN : Spotlight, 2019 |
   Series: Star Wars: Darth Vader Set 3 | Volume 1 written by Kieron Gillen;
   illustrated by Leinil Francis Yu, Gerry Alanguilan and Jason Keith. | Volumes 2-5
   written by Kieron Gillen; illustrated by Salvador Larroca and Edgar Delgado.
Summary: The ore-rich planet of Shu-Torun is revolting. And there's no way the
   Empire will stand for that. Darth Vader is tasked with leading a military assault
   against the planet. Could it be his rise to glory? And who will follow him into
   battle? It's better to fight alongside Vader than against him, and that's a lesson
   the Ore Barons are about to learn.
Identifiers: LCCN 2017961399 | ISBN 9781532141621 (Volume 1) | ISBN
   9781532141638 (Volume 2) | ISBN 9781532141645 (Volume 3) | ISBN
   9781532141652 (Volume 4) | ISBN 9781532141669 (Volume 5)
Subjects: LCSH: Star Wars films--Juvenile fiction. | Vader, Darth (Fictitious
   character)--Juvenile fiction. | Space colonies--Juvenile fiction. | Imaginary wars
   and battles--Juvenile fiction. | Comic books, strips, etc.--Juvenile fiction.
Classification: DDC 741.5--dc23
LC record available at http://lccn.loc.gov/2017961399

Spotlight

A Division of ABDO
abdopublishing.com

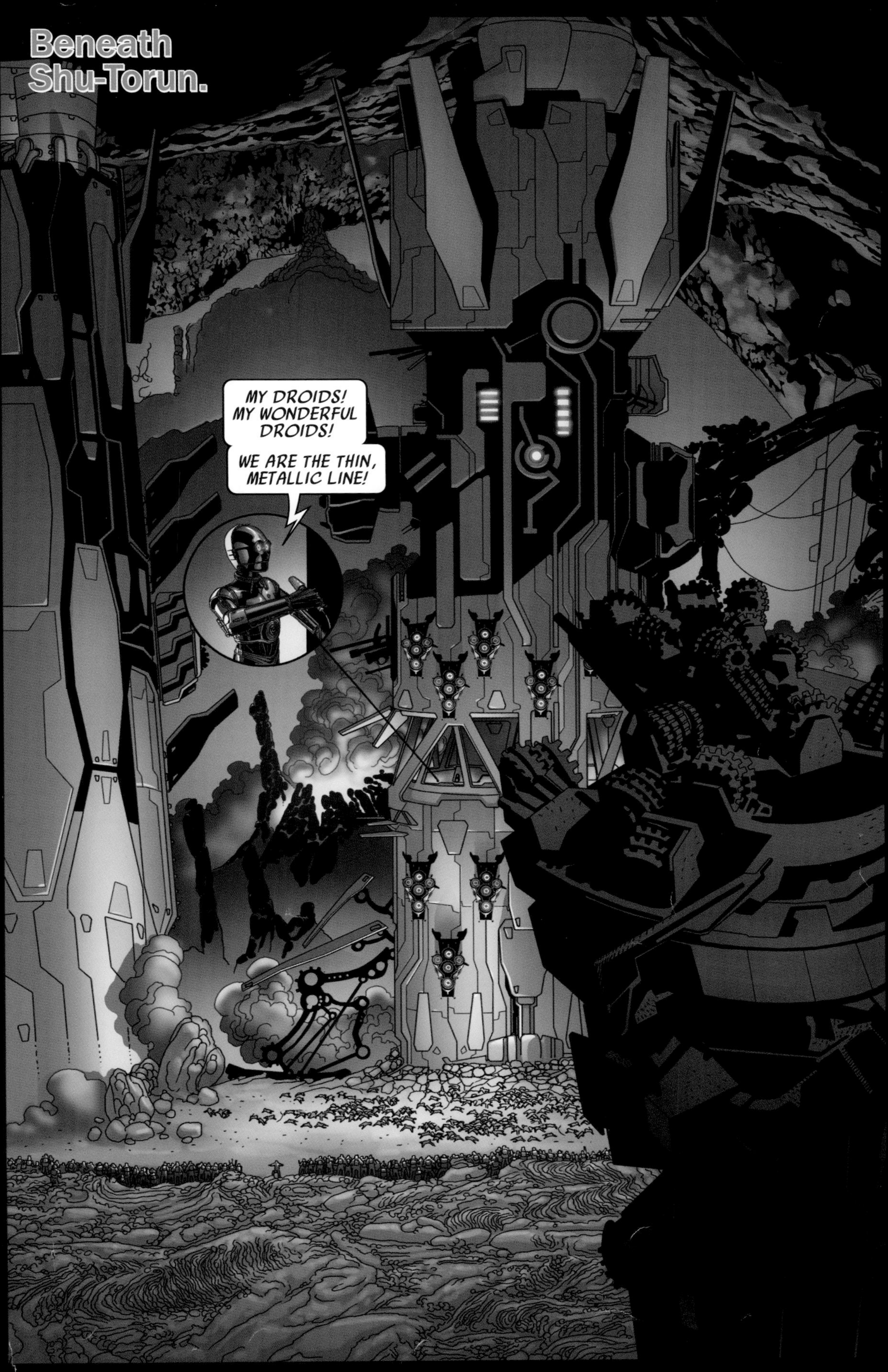
Beneath Shu-Torun.
MY DROIDS! MY WONDERFUL DROIDS!
WE ARE THE THIN, METALLIC LINE!

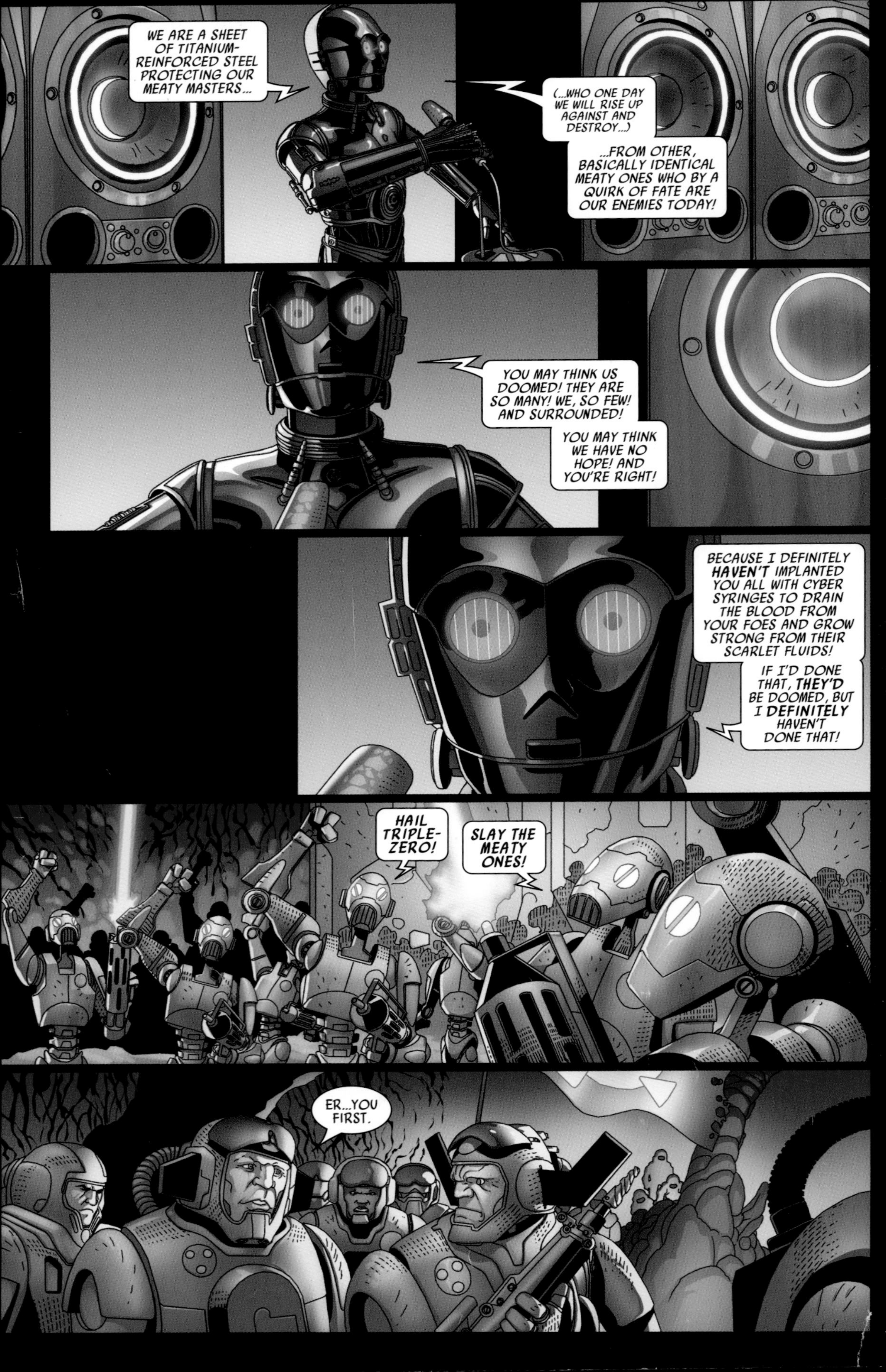
WE ARE A SHEET OF TITANIUM-REINFORCED STEEL PROTECTING OUR MEATY MASTERS...
(...WHO ONE DAY WE WILL RISE UP AGAINST AND DESTROY...)
...FROM OTHER, BASICALLY IDENTICAL MEATY ONES WHO BY A QUIRK OF FATE ARE OUR ENEMIES TODAY!
YOU MAY THINK US DOOMED! THEY ARE SO MANY! WE, SO FEW! AND SURROUNDED!
YOU MAY THINK WE HAVE NO HOPE! AND YOU'RE RIGHT!
BECAUSE I DEFINITELY HAVEN'T IMPLANTED YOU ALL WITH CYBER SYRINGES TO DRAIN THE BLOOD FROM YOUR FOES AND GROW STRONG FROM THEIR SCARLET FLUIDS!
IF I'D DONE THAT, THEY'D BE DOOMED, BUT I DEFINITELY HAVEN'T DONE THAT!
HAIL TRIPLE-ZERO!
SLAY THE MEATY ONES!
ER...YOU FIRST.

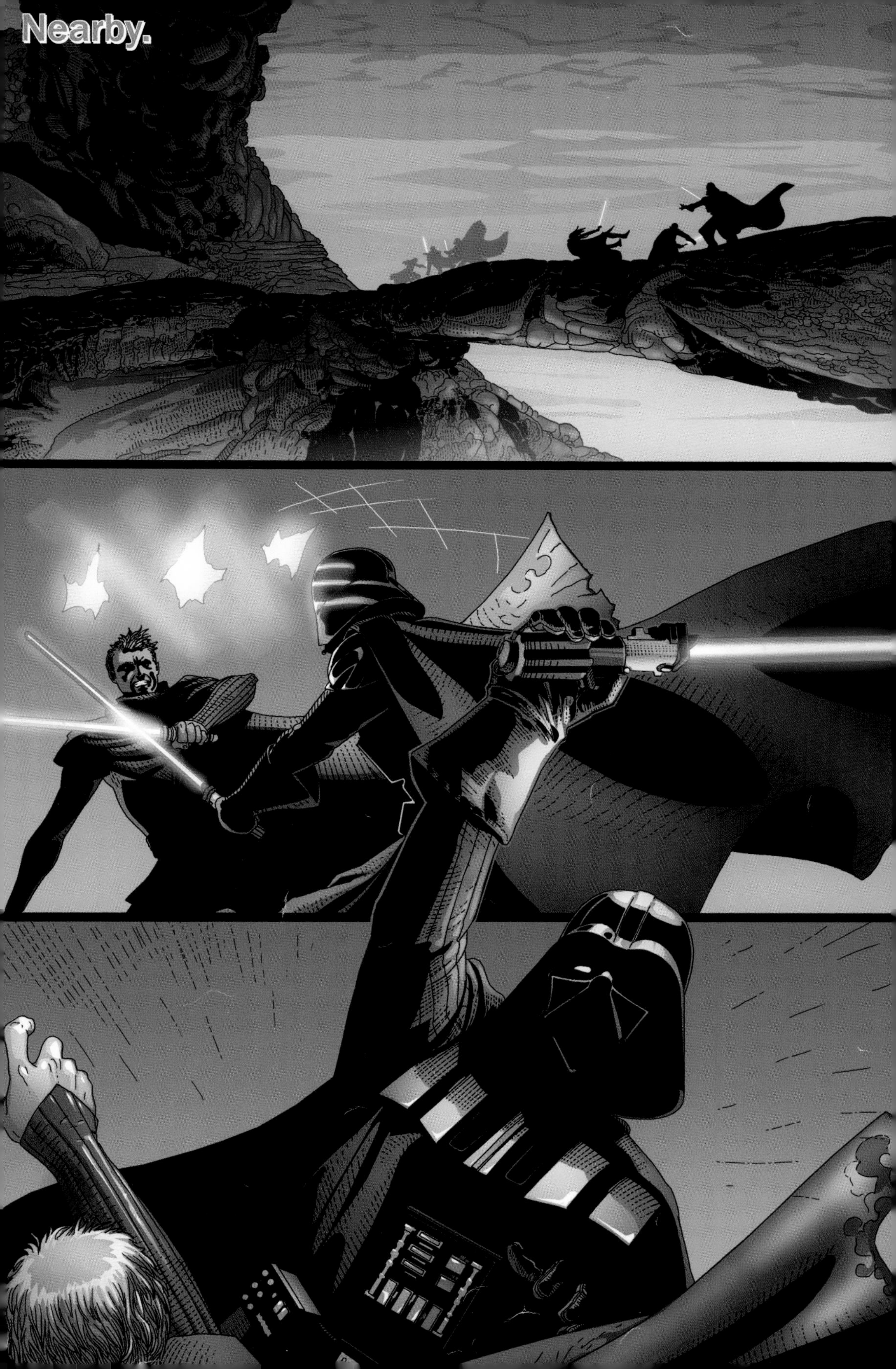
Nearby.

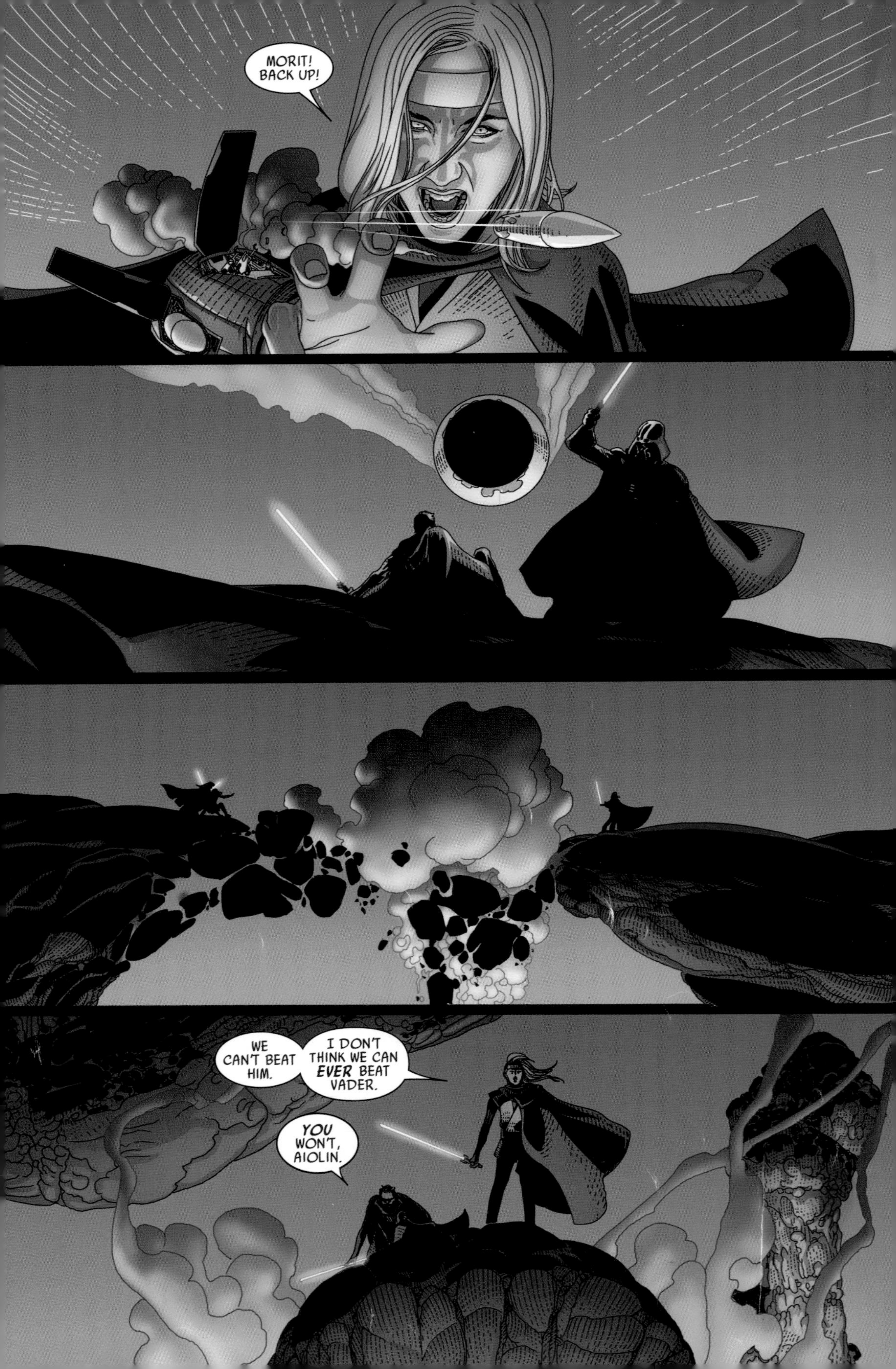
MORIT! BACK UP!
WE CAN'T BEAT HIM.
I DON'T THINK WE CAN EVER BEAT VADER.
YOU WON'T, AIOLIN.

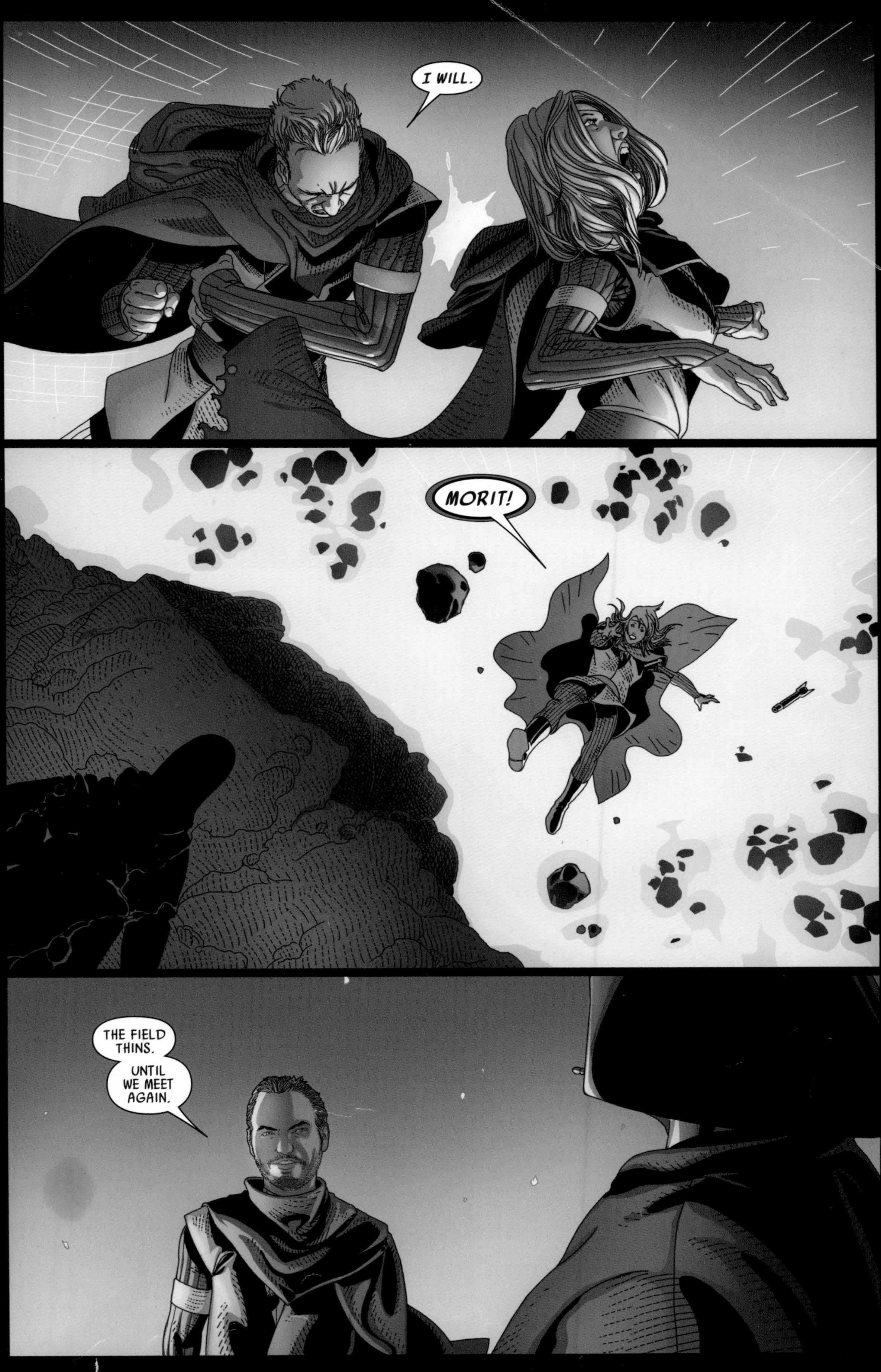
I WILL.
MORIT!
THE FIELD THINS.
UNTIL WE MEET AGAIN.

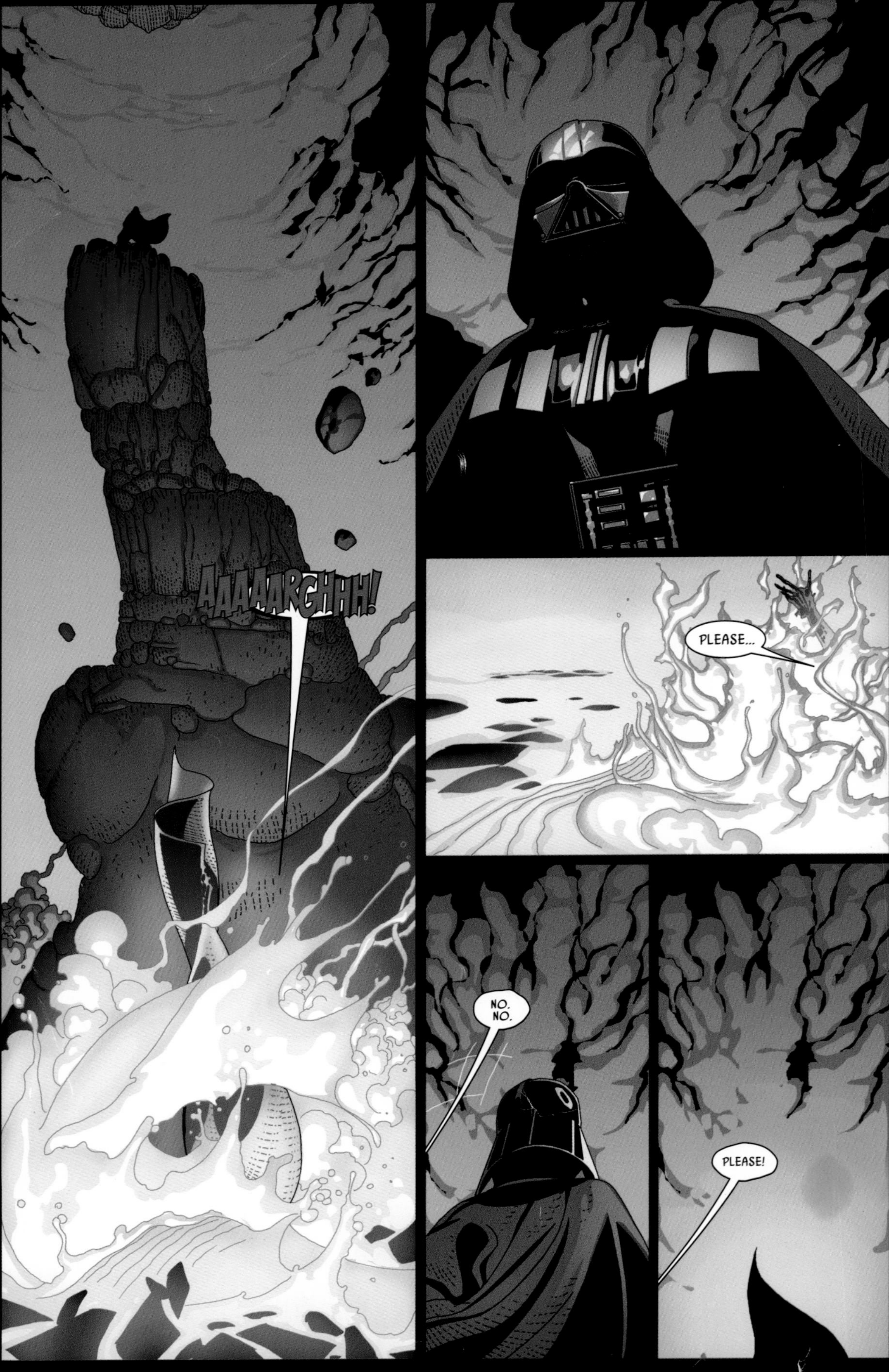
AAAAARGHHH!
PLEASE...
NO. NO.
PLEASE!

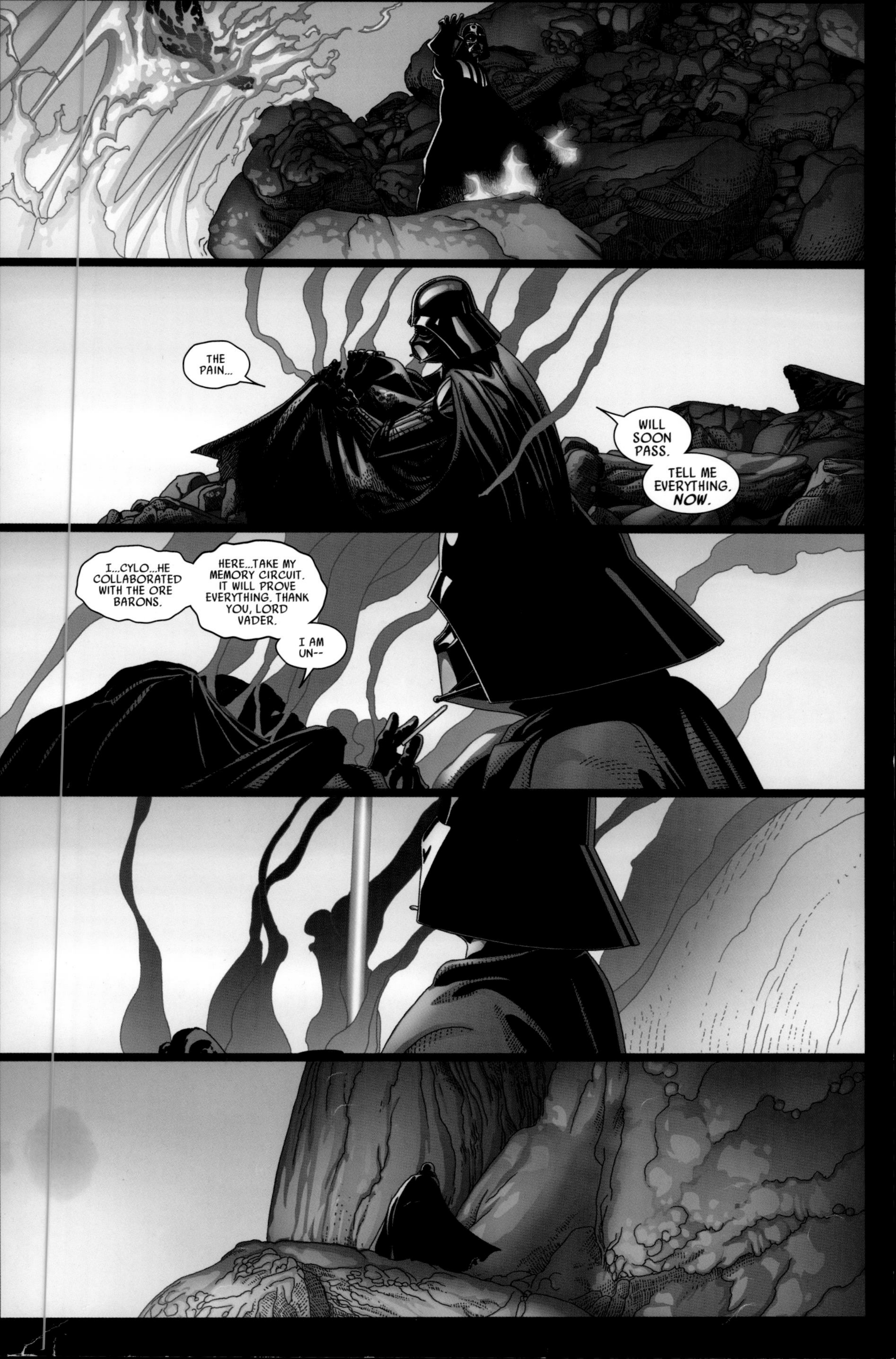
THE PAIN...
WILL SOON PASS.
TELL ME EVERYTHING. NOW.
I...CYLO...HE COLLABORATED WITH THE ORE BARONS.
HERE...TAKE MY MEMORY CIRCUIT. IT WILL PROVE EVERYTHING. THANK YOU, LORD VADER.
I AM UN--

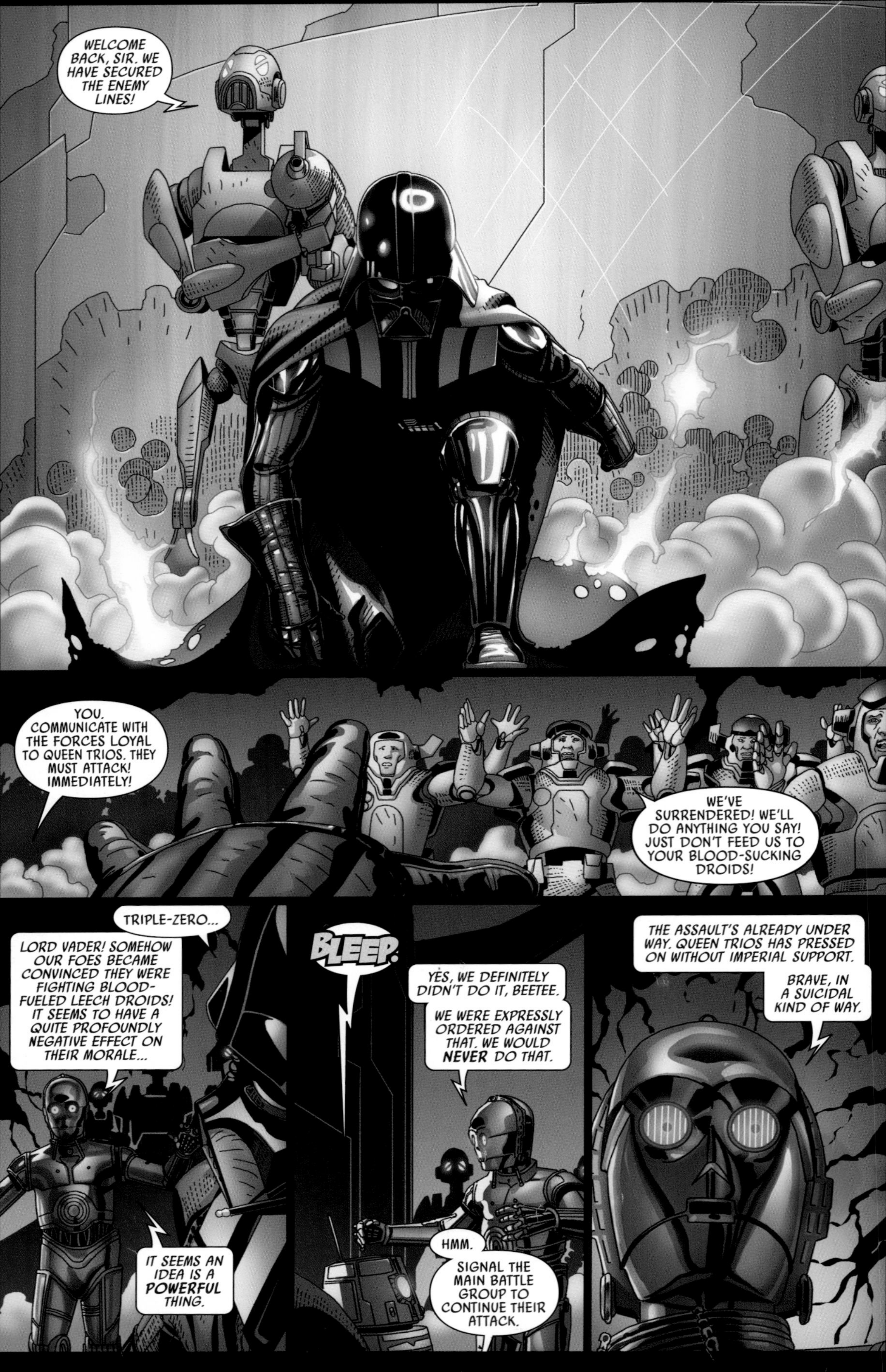
WELCOME BACK, SIR. WE HAVE SECURED THE ENEMY LINES!
YOU. COMMUNICATE WITH THE FORCES LOYAL TO QUEEN TRIOS. THEY MUST ATTACK! IMMEDIATELY!
WE'VE SURRENDERED! WE'LL DO ANYTHING YOU SAY! JUST DON'T FEED US TO YOUR BLOOD-SUCKING DROIDS!
TRIPLE-ZERO...
LORD VADER! SOMEHOW OUR FOES BECAME CONVINCED THEY WERE FIGHTING BLOOD-FUELED LEECH DROIDS! IT SEEMS TO HAVE A QUITE PROFOUNDLY NEGATIVE EFFECT ON THEIR MORALE...
IT SEEMS AN IDEA IS A **POWERFUL** THING.
BLEEP!
YES, WE DEFINITELY DIDN'T DO IT, BEETEE.
WE WERE EXPRESSLY ORDERED AGAINST THAT. WE WOULD **NEVER** DO THAT.
HMM.
SIGNAL THE MAIN BATTLE GROUP TO CONTINUE THEIR ATTACK.
THE ASSAULT'S ALREADY UNDER WAY. QUEEN TRIOS HAS PRESSED ON WITHOUT IMPERIAL SUPPORT.
BRAVE, IN A SUICIDAL KIND OF WAY.

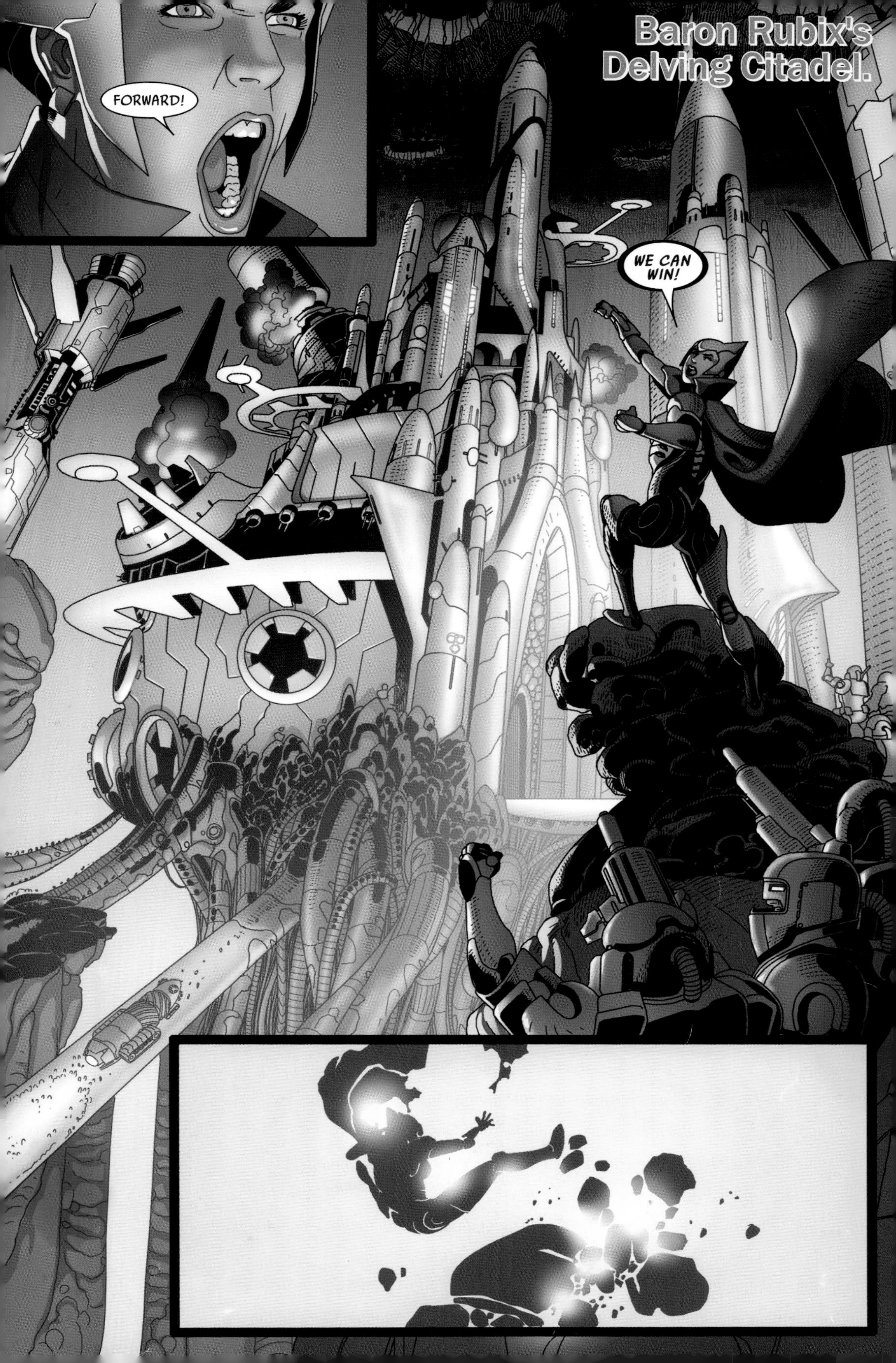
FORWARD!
Baron Rubix's Delving Citadel.
WE CAN WIN!

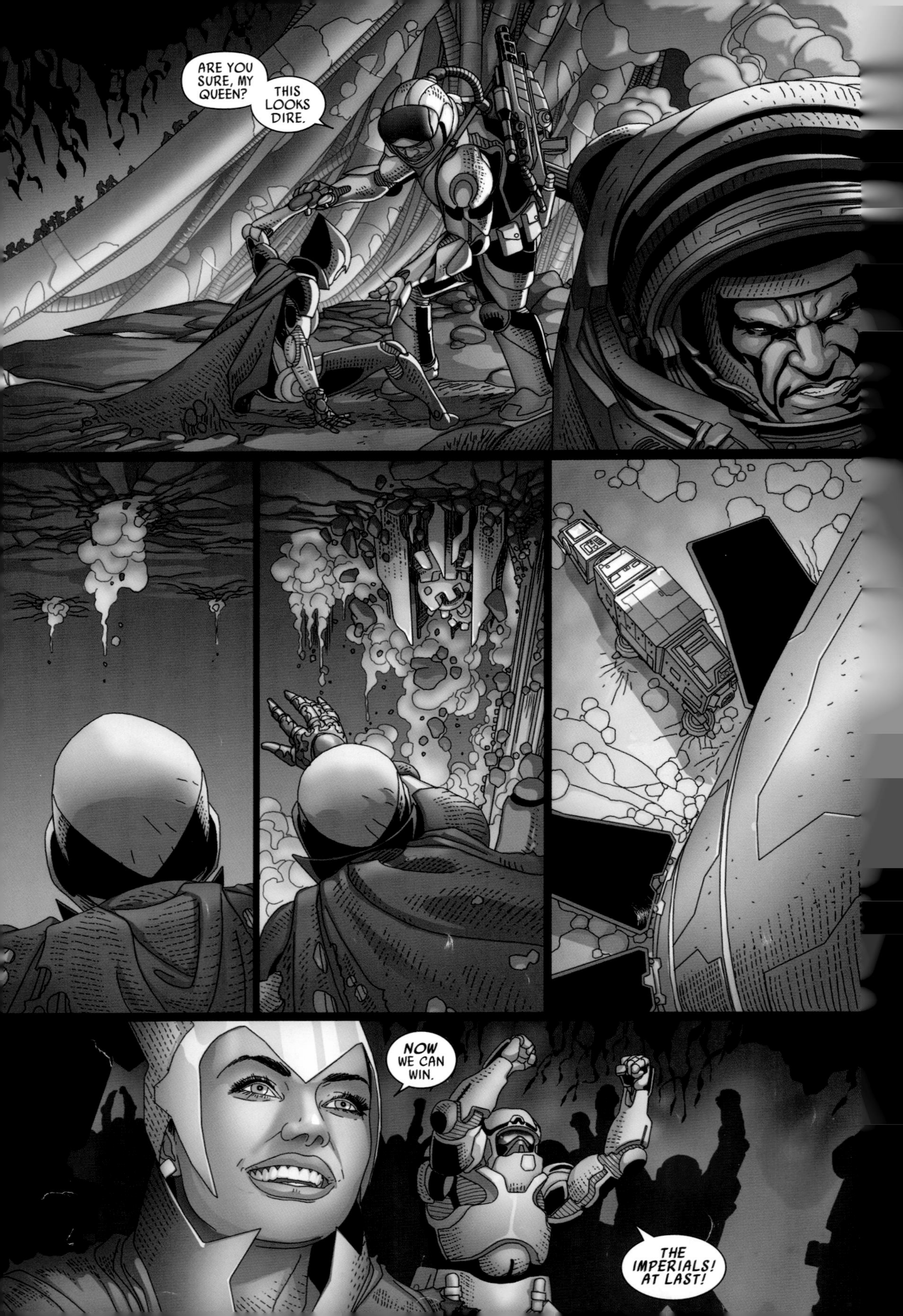

ARE YOU SURE, MY QUEEN?
THIS LOOKS DIRE.
NOW WE CAN WIN.
THE IMPERIALS! AT LAST!

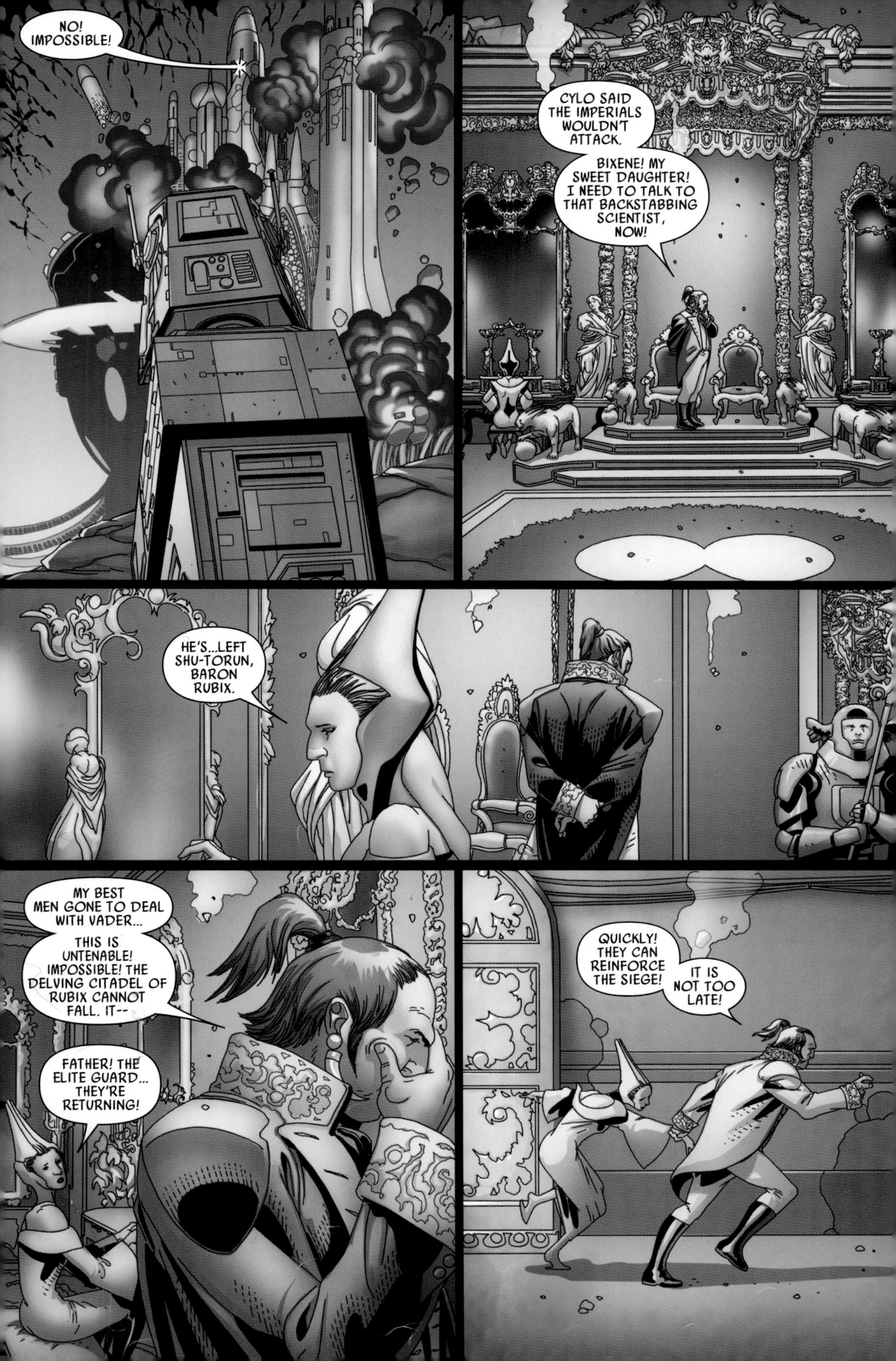
NO! IMPOSSIBLE!
CYLO SAID THE IMPERIALS WOULDN'T ATTACK.
BIXENE! MY SWEET DAUGHTER! I NEED TO TALK TO THAT BACKSTABBING SCIENTIST, NOW!
HE'S...LEFT SHU-TORUN, BARON RUBIX.
MY BEST MEN GONE TO DEAL WITH VADER...
THIS IS UNTENABLE! IMPOSSIBLE! THE DELVING CITADEL OF RUBIX CANNOT FALL. IT--
FATHER! THE ELITE GUARD... THEY'RE RETURNING!
QUICKLY! THEY CAN REINFORCE THE SIEGE!
IT IS NOT TOO LATE!

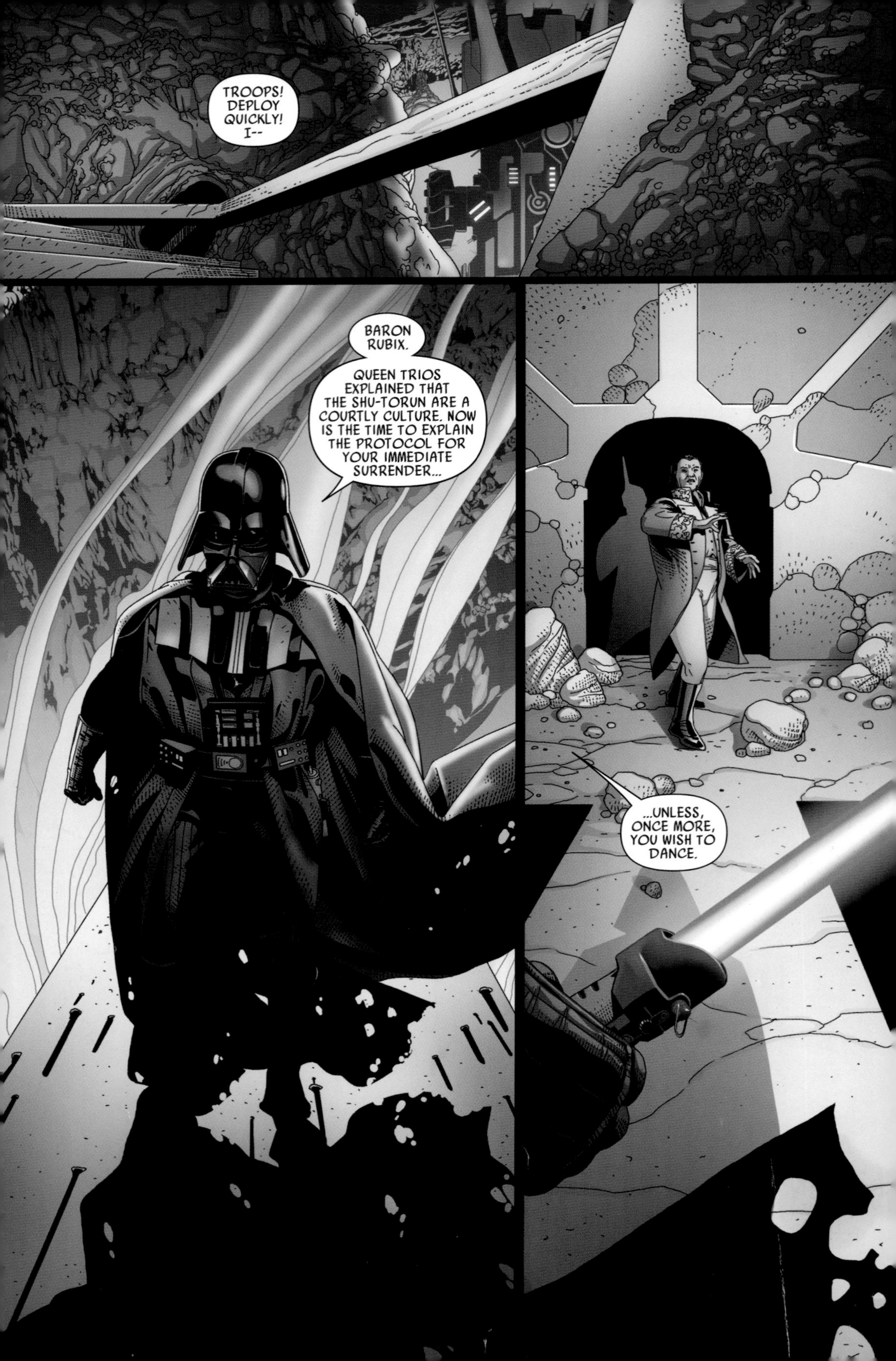
TROOPS! DEPLOY QUICKLY! I--
BARON RUBIX.
QUEEN TRIOS EXPLAINED THAT THE SHU-TORUN ARE A COURTLY CULTURE. NOW IS THE TIME TO EXPLAIN THE PROTOCOL FOR YOUR IMMEDIATE SURRENDER...
...UNLESS, ONCE MORE, YOU WISH TO DANCE.

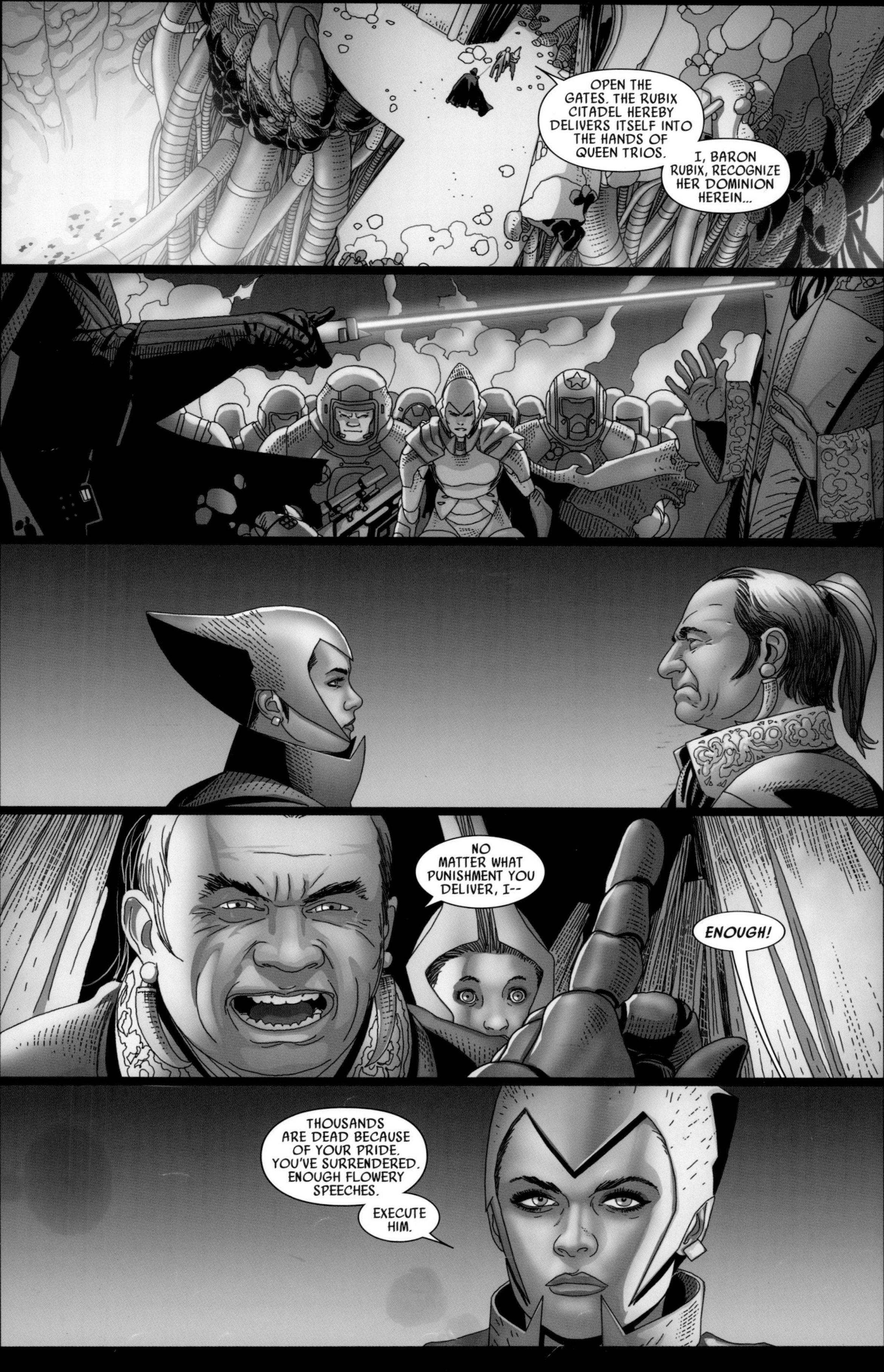
OPEN THE GATES. THE RUBIX CITADEL HEREBY DELIVERS ITSELF INTO THE HANDS OF QUEEN TRIOS.
I, BARON RUBIX, RECOGNIZE HER DOMINION HEREIN...
NO MATTER WHAT PUNISHMENT YOU DELIVER, I--
ENOUGH!
THOUSANDS ARE DEAD BECAUSE OF YOUR PRIDE. YOU'VE SURRENDERED. ENOUGH FLOWERY SPEECHES.
EXECUTE HIM.

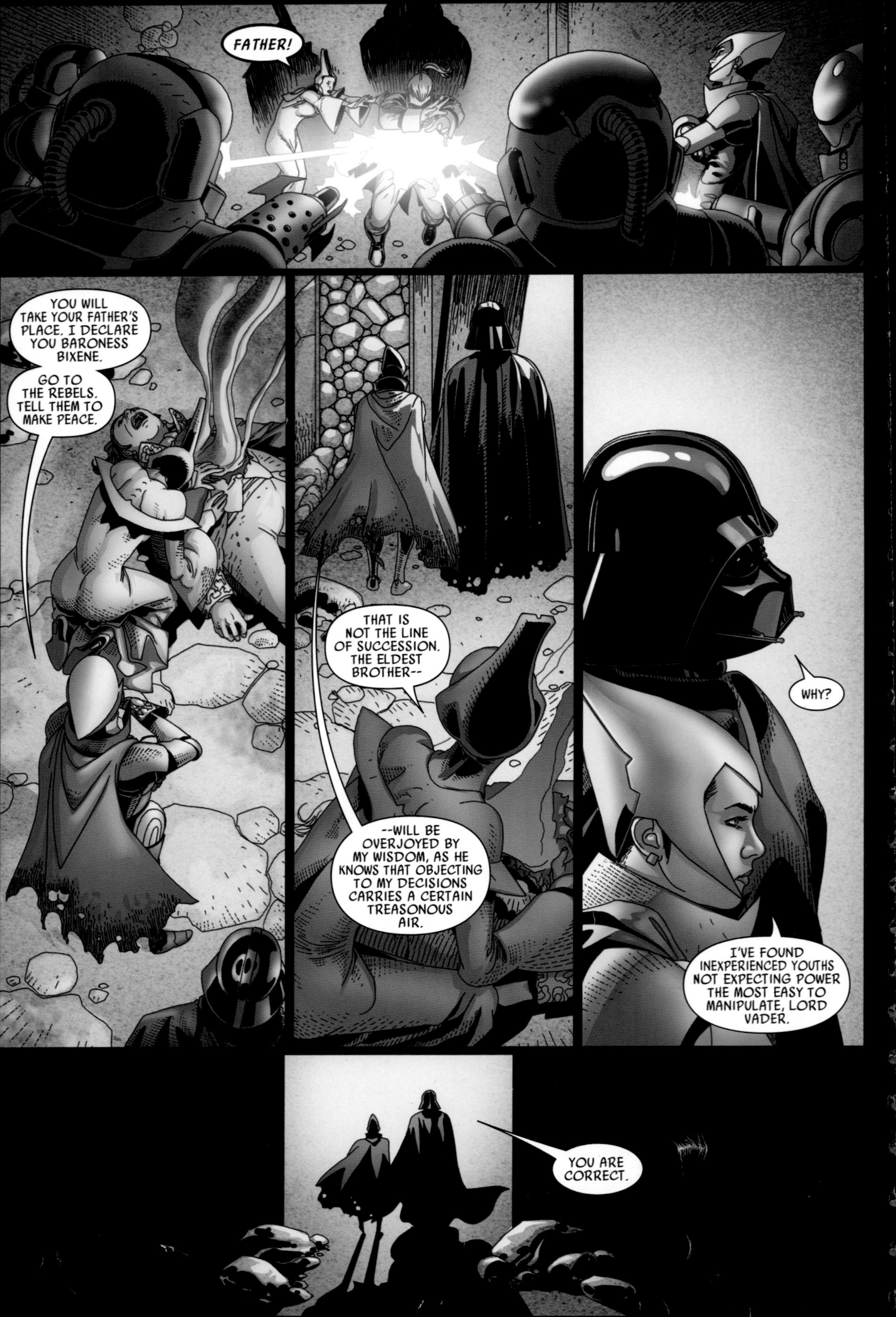
FATHER!
YOU WILL TAKE YOUR FATHER'S PLACE. I DECLARE YOU BARONESS BIXENE.
GO TO THE REBELS. TELL THEM TO MAKE PEACE.
THAT IS NOT THE LINE OF SUCCESSION. THE ELDEST BROTHER--
--WILL BE OVERJOYED BY MY WISDOM, AS HE KNOWS THAT OBJECTING TO MY DECISIONS CARRIES A CERTAIN TREASONOUS AIR.
WHY?
I'VE FOUND INEXPERIENCED YOUTHS NOT EXPECTING POWER THE MOST EASY TO MANIPULATE, LORD VADER.
YOU ARE CORRECT.

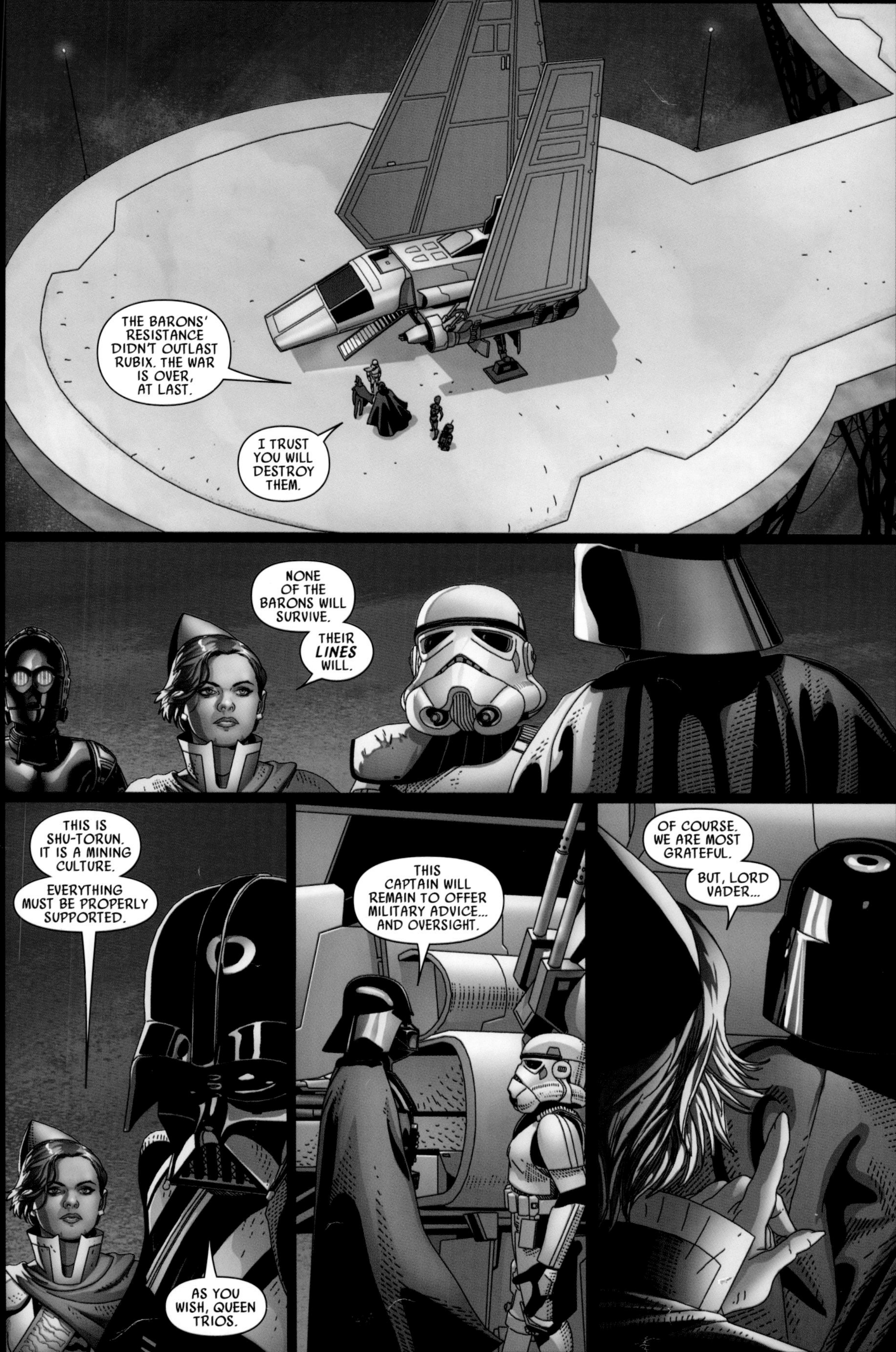
THE BARONS' RESISTANCE DIDN'T OUTLAST RUBIX. THE WAR IS OVER, AT LAST.
I TRUST YOU WILL DESTROY THEM.
NONE OF THE BARONS WILL SURVIVE.
THEIR *LINES* WILL.
THIS IS SHU-TORUN. IT IS A MINING CULTURE.
EVERYTHING MUST BE PROPERLY SUPPORTED.
AS YOU WISH, QUEEN TRIOS.
THIS CAPTAIN WILL REMAIN TO OFFER MILITARY ADVICE... AND OVERSIGHT.
OF COURSE. WE ARE MOST GRATEFUL.
BUT, LORD VADER...

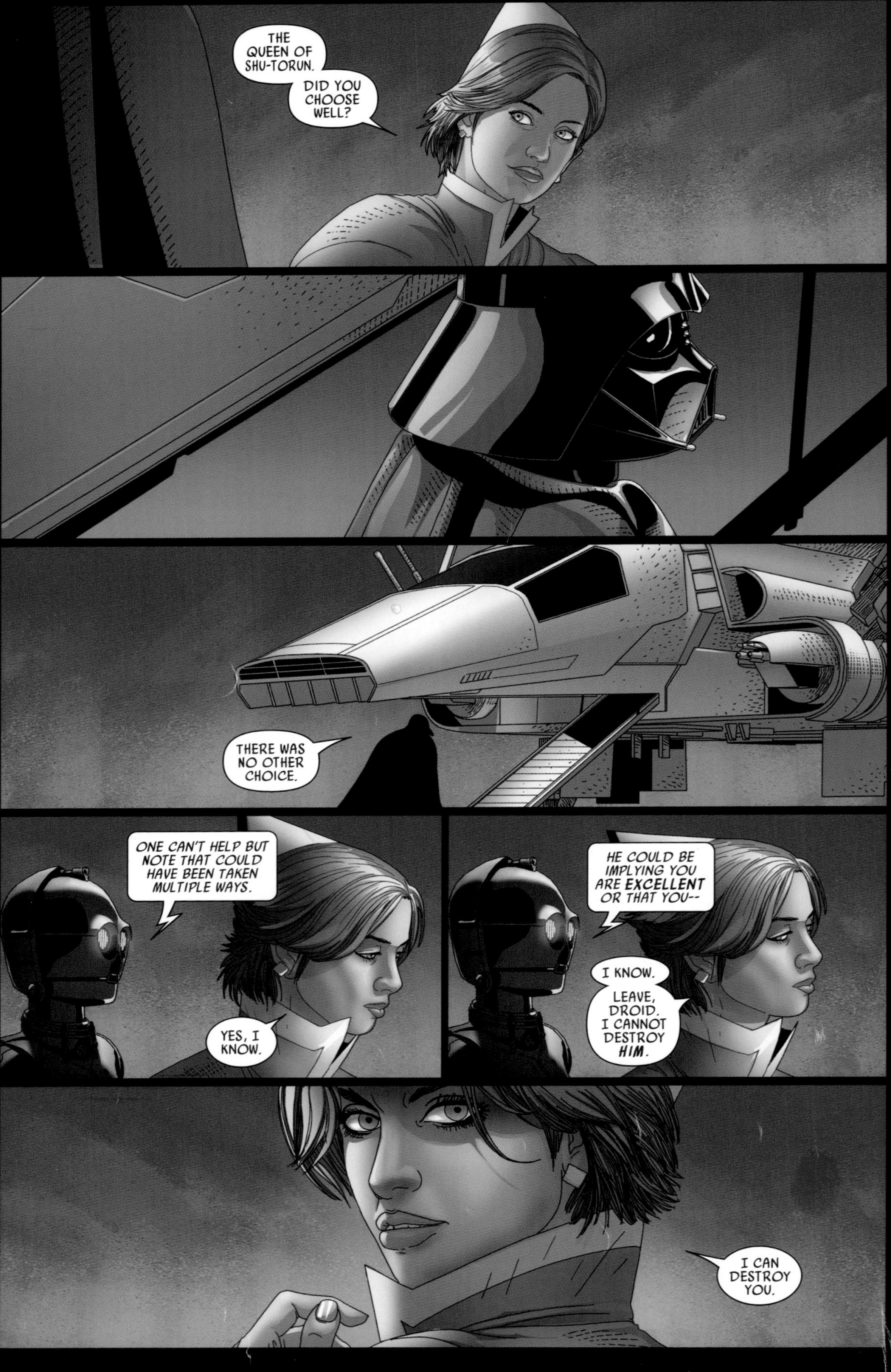
THE QUEEN OF SHU-TORUN.
DID YOU CHOOSE WELL?
THERE WAS NO OTHER CHOICE.
ONE CAN'T HELP BUT NOTE THAT COULD HAVE BEEN TAKEN MULTIPLE WAYS.
YES, I KNOW.
HE COULD BE IMPLYING YOU ARE **EXCELLENT** OR THAT YOU--
I KNOW.
LEAVE, DROID. I CANNOT DESTROY ***HIM***.
I CAN DESTROY YOU.

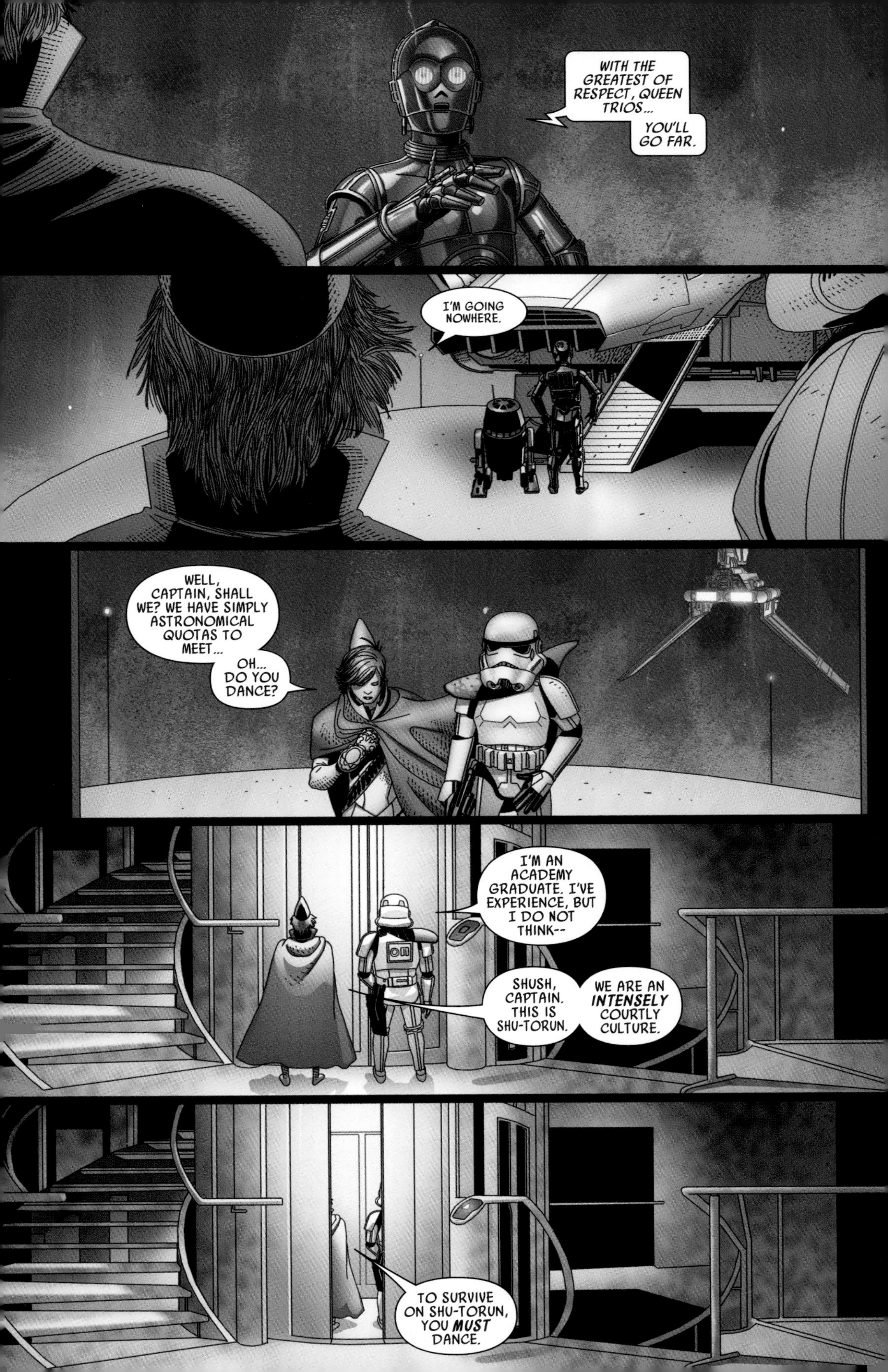
WITH THE GREATEST OF RESPECT, QUEEN TRIOS...
YOU'LL GO FAR.
I'M GOING NOWHERE.
WELL, CAPTAIN, SHALL WE? WE HAVE SIMPLY ASTRONOMICAL QUOTAS TO MEET...
OH... DO YOU DANCE?
I'M AN ACADEMY GRADUATE. I'VE EXPERIENCE, BUT I DO NOT THINK--
SHUSH, CAPTAIN. THIS IS SHU-TORUN.
WE ARE AN INTENSELY COURTLY CULTURE.
TO SURVIVE ON SHU-TORUN, YOU MUST DANCE.

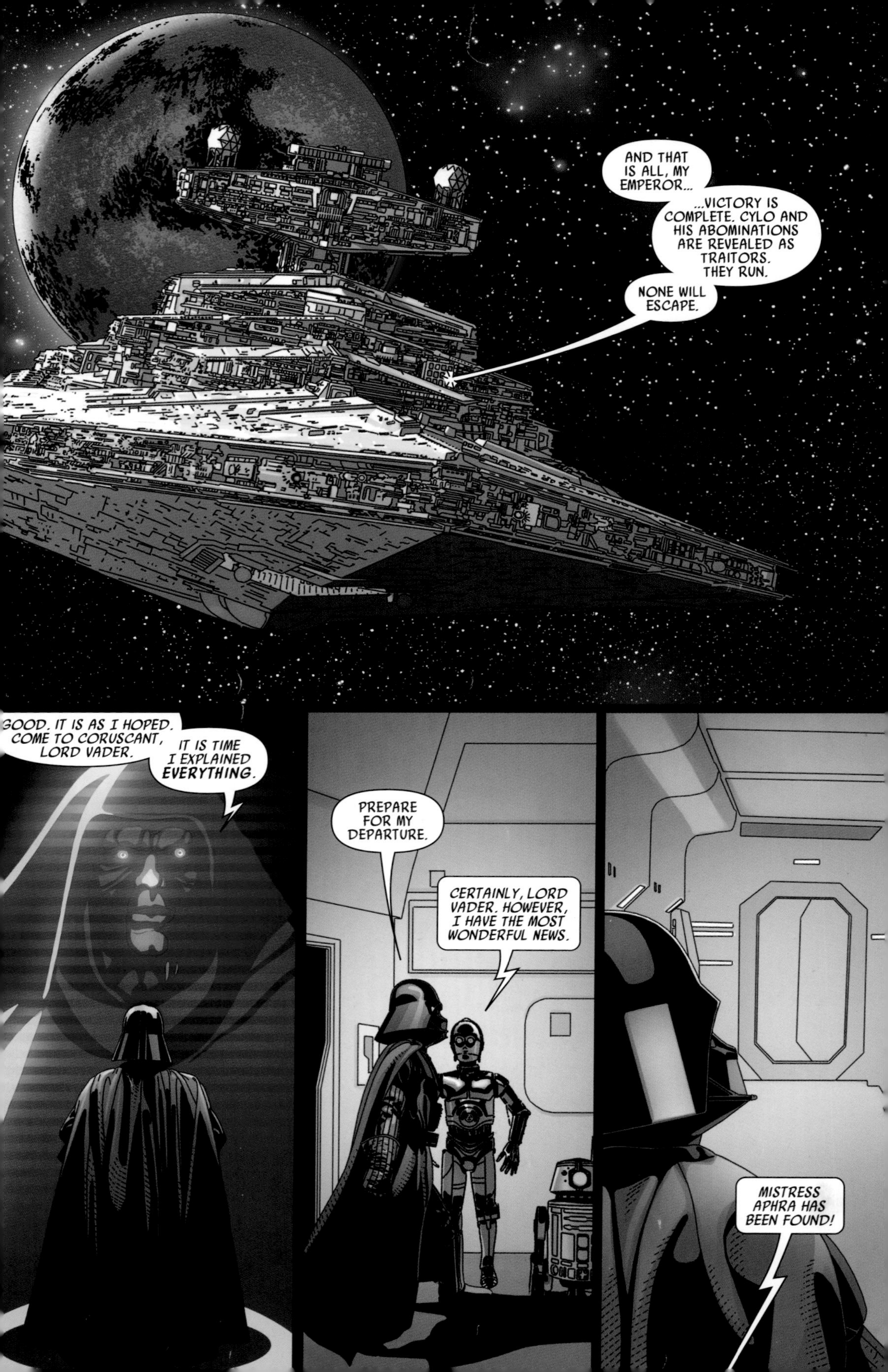
AND THAT IS ALL, MY EMPEROR...
...VICTORY IS COMPLETE. CYLO AND HIS ABOMINATIONS ARE REVEALED AS TRAITORS. THEY RUN.
NONE WILL ESCAPE.
GOOD. IT IS AS I HOPED. COME TO CORUSCANT, LORD VADER.
IT IS TIME I EXPLAINED **EVERYTHING**.
PREPARE FOR MY DEPARTURE.
CERTAINLY, LORD VADER. HOWEVER, I HAVE THE MOST WONDERFUL NEWS.
MISTRESS APHRA HAS BEEN FOUND!

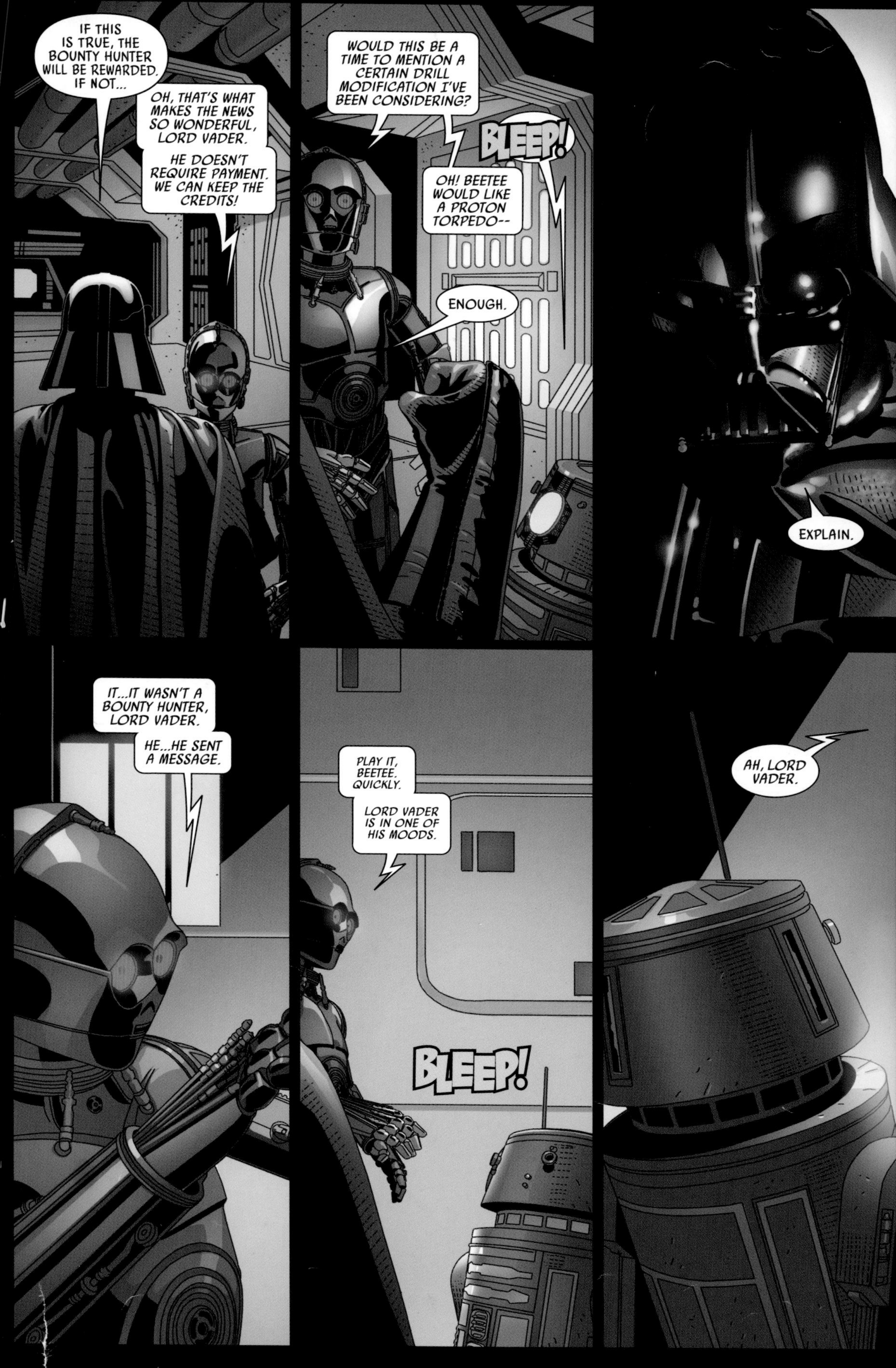
IF THIS IS TRUE, THE BOUNTY HUNTER WILL BE REWARDED. IF NOT...
OH, THAT'S WHAT MAKES THE NEWS SO WONDERFUL, LORD VADER.
HE DOESN'T REQUIRE PAYMENT. WE CAN KEEP THE CREDITS!
WOULD THIS BE A TIME TO MENTION A CERTAIN DRILL MODIFICATION I'VE BEEN CONSIDERING?
BLEEP!
OH! BEETEE WOULD LIKE A PROTON TORPEDO--
ENOUGH.
EXPLAIN.
IT...IT WASN'T A BOUNTY HUNTER, LORD VADER.
HE...HE SENT A MESSAGE.
PLAY IT, BEETEE. QUICKLY.
LORD VADER IS IN ONE OF HIS MOODS.
BLEEP!
AH, LORD VADER.

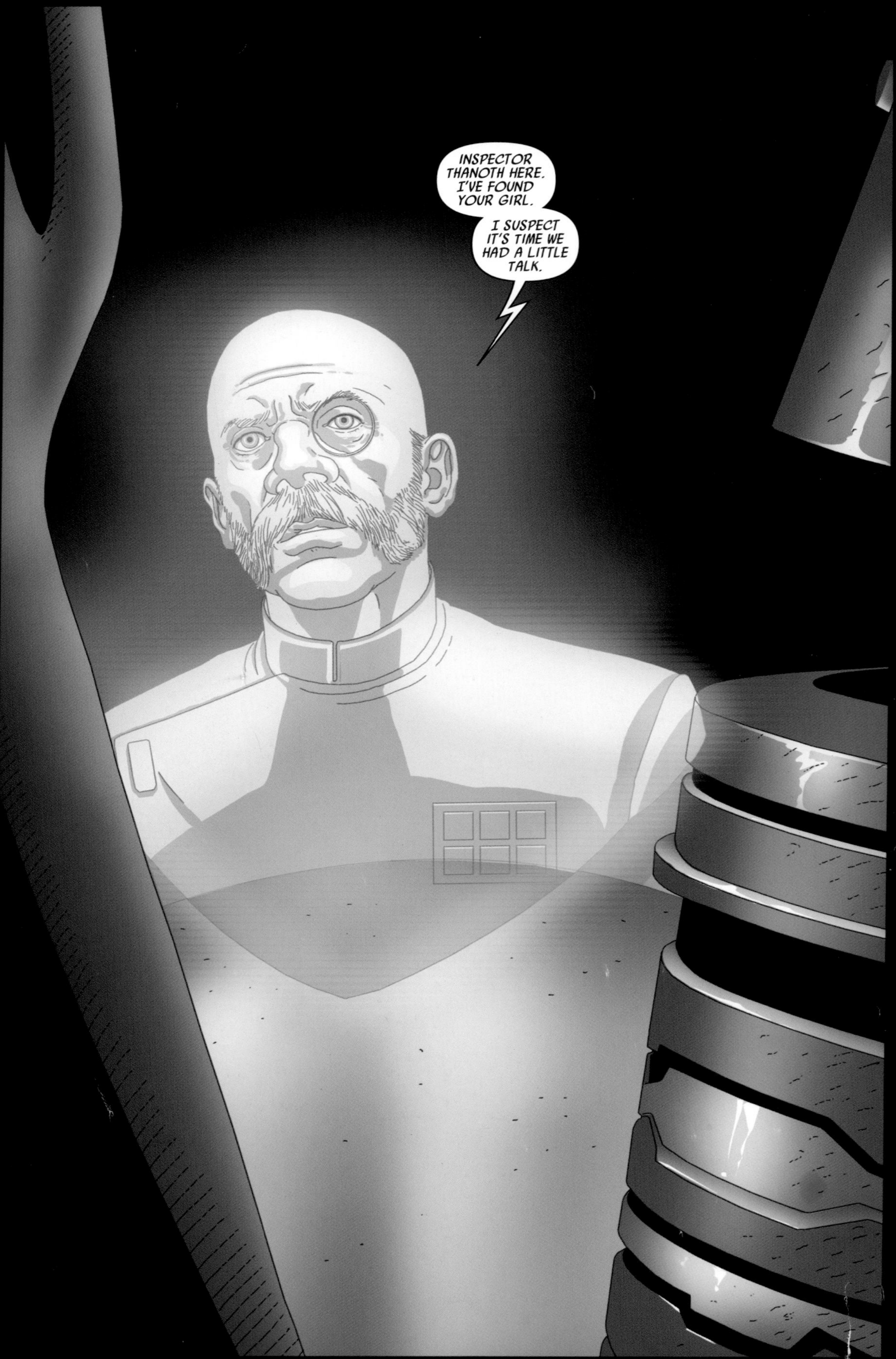
INSPECTOR THANOTH HERE. I'VE FOUND YOUR GIRL.
I SUSPECT IT'S TIME WE HAD A LITTLE TALK.

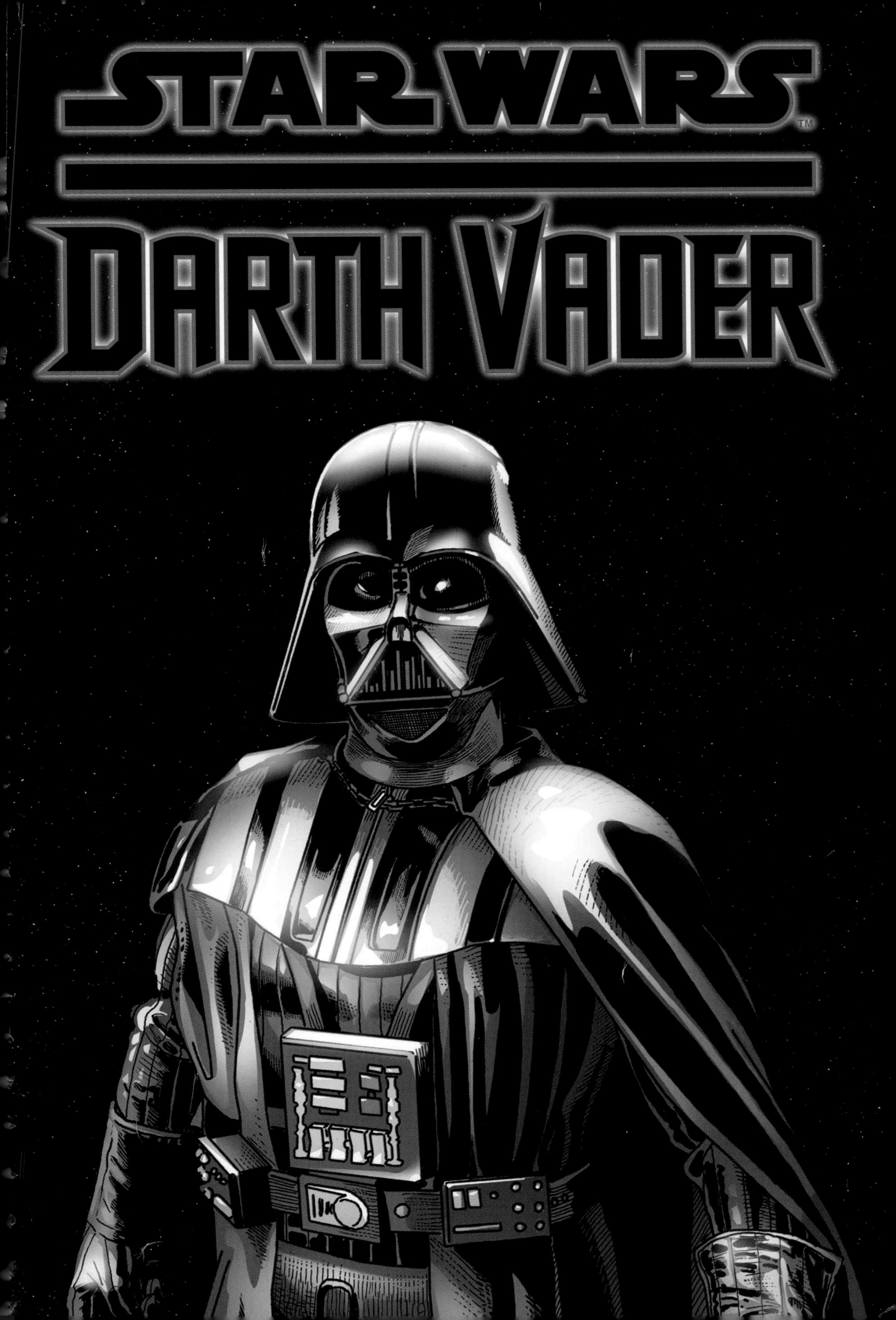
STAR WARS
DARTH VADER

STAR WARS
DARTH VADER

COLLECT THEM ALL!

Set of 5 Hardcover Books ISBN: 978-1-5321-4161-4

STAR WARS
STAR WARS
DARTH VADER
THE SHU-TORUN WAR: VOLUME 1
GILLEN YU ALANGUILAN KEITH

Hardcover Book ISBN
978-1-5321-4162-1

STAR WARS
STAR WARS
DARTH VADER
THE SHU-TORUN WAR: VOLUME 2
GILLEN LARROCA DELGADO

Hardcover Book ISBN
978-1-5321-4163-8

STAR WARS
STAR WARS
DARTH VADER
THE SHU-TORUN WAR: VOLUME 3
GILLEN LARROCA DELGADO

Hardcover Book ISBN
978-1-5321-4164-5

STAR WARS
STAR WARS
DARTH VADER
THE SHU-TORUN WAR: VOLUME 4
GILLEN LARROCA DELGADO

Hardcover Book ISBN
978-1-5321-4165-2

STAR WARS
STAR WARS
DARTH VADER
THE SHU-TORUN WAR: VOLUME 5
GILLEN LARROCA DELGADO

Hardcover Book ISBN
978-1-5321-4166-9

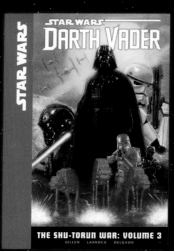

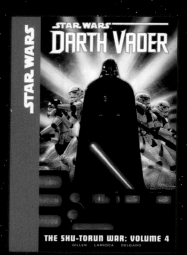

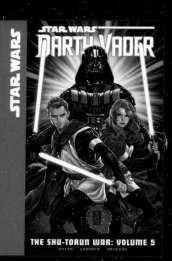

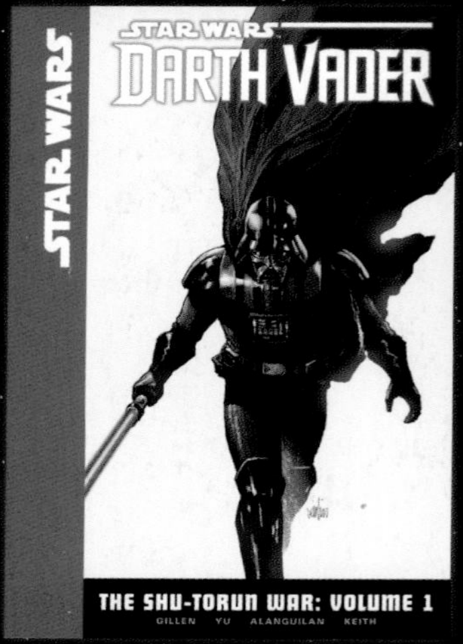

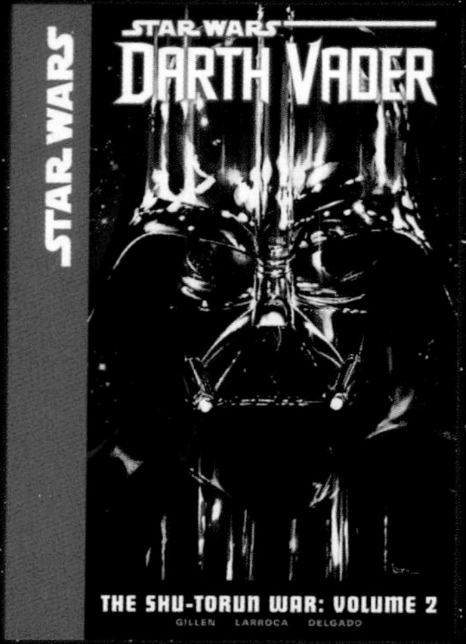